Making Healthy Choices

A Story to Inspire Fit, Weight-Wise Kids

BOYS' EDITION

By Merilee A. Kern, MBA
Edited by Lori Sellstrom
Illustrated by Jerry DeCrotie

It's Not Your Fault That You're Overweight
A Story to Inspire Fit, Weight-Wise Kids (Boys' Edition)

Published by Starbound Books™
610 East Delano Street, Suite 104, Tucson, Arizona 85705 U.S.A.
www.starboundbooks.com

ISBN-10: 1-58736-742-4
ISBN-13: 978-1-58736-742-7
LCCN: 2006937435

For Ron, Mason, and Devyn, with all my love – M.K.

Special thanks to Susan Burke, MS, RD, LD/N, CDE, whose invaluable insights, opinions, and suggestions helped make this book a powerful tool for the many children struggling with weight issues.

TABLE OF CONTENTS

PREFACE

Parents, you are encouraged to read this story aloud with your child so that you can key in on those specific experiences that resonate with him. Generally, it's expected that the majority of overweight or obese boys will relate to one or more of Matt's "bad choices," as well as the implications of being an overweight child from a social perspective. This book portrays the most common struggles and concerns from Matt's 10-year-old perspective. If you have yet to establish dialogue with your child regarding his health, or are simply at your wit's end having seemingly "tried it all," this fictional tale offers a non-combative opportunity for your child to see that someone *does* understand his struggle and that relatively easy changes can be made that WILL result in a better lifestyle.

Why is this book important? Consider these alarming statistics: The Centers For Disease Control and Prevention (CDC) reports that an estimated 65 percent of U.S. adults are either overweight or obese, and over 20 percent of American children are as well. Unfortunately, these numbers continue to rise. The prevalence of obesity among children in the United States increased by 100 percent between 1980 and 1994, and half of all Americans—and most adolescents—drink sugar-laden soda daily. In addition, studies have found that a staggering 88.5 percent of the foods sold in student stores are high in fat and/or sugar. This combined with the overall decrease in kids' physical activity, the increase in sedentary time spent in front of the television, computer, or video games, and the increased incidence of type 2 diabetes among children, spells danger for the future health of our children . . . and our nation, both medically and economically.

We **must** help our children recognize the overwhelming amount of cultural influences that adversely impact their decision making, and lessen the emotional burden carried by children who have internalized sole responsibility for their weight problem. Rather than harboring displaced blame or guilt, our kids would greatly benefit from re-focusing their emotional and physical energy on making positive, healthful changes in their lives.

FOREWORD

We live in a time when childhood obesity is reaching epic proportions, as are the typical food servings dished up to our nation's youth—much to their naive delight. The old adage remains true: ignorance is bliss, but it's time for our children to get educated on the relationship of lifestyle and health! A method of teaching children how to recognize and circumvent negative societal influences, while also imparting how and why to make better lifestyle choices, is long overdue, and *It's Not Your Fault That You're Overweight* has addressed this glaring need in a compassionate and understanding style that is sure to connect with the reader.

True learning happens when children identify with the lesson at hand, as they will cognitively "shut down" if they perceive any kind of threat. This book effectively employs non-confrontational methodology to present this vital subject, and actually lifts displaced self-blame off kids' shoulders. With this emotional burden removed, overweight and obese boys will relate to, empathize with, and feel inspired by Matt—their fictional peer.

Not just for those struggling with weight issues, children everywhere will delight in following Matt's journey to a fitter, healthier, and happier life. Experiencing the problems of an adolescent overweight condition through Matt's eyes, and watching him ultimately triumph over the various challenges to achieve good health, allows children to not only better understand why they need to adopt healthy behaviors, but also to realize exactly how to do it and the rewards that will ensue. With this book, Merilee Kern has created a viable tool in our fight against America's burgeoning "epidemic of obesity." I herald this intervention intended to help our kids live healthier and more fulfilling lives through a fun, example driven, and moderate approach to weight control. If you know an adolescent struggling with a weight problem, *It's Not Your Fault That You're Overweight* is one of the most important gifts you could possibly give—the gift of hope.

Julia Havey
Motivational speaker and author of
Awaken the Diet Within, LifeChanger, and *The Vice Busting Diet*

Chapter 1

Negative Influences . . . Poor Choices

This is Matt. He's a funny and smart 10-year-old who likes to sing, play with his dog Skipper, and go to the movies with his friends. Matt also likes to eat. Sometimes Matt eats too much, and he often chooses to eat sugary and fatty foods that are not very nutritious. He doesn't exercise much, either. These poor choices have made Matt weigh more than he should, putting his health at risk. It's not Matt's fault, though. He just doesn't realize that he's actually being encouraged to make bad choices by the world around him. He also doesn't know that weighing too much can be dangerous to his health.

Matt wisely eats a breakfast each morning that his mom happily prepares for the two of them. Some days Matt eats a big stack of pancakes with lots of butter and maple syrup on top. Other days he eats a bacon, egg, and cheese sandwich on a buttered roll. Sometimes he just eats a couple of chocolate covered donuts with milk, or one of those fruity marshmallow crunch cereals that have a neat toy in the box.

Matt often eats his breakfast and other meals in front of the TV so that he doesn't miss his favorite shows, or his three favorite commercials. One commercial has a really funny hamburger and French fries telling jokes to each other. Another one shows "cool" kids surfing on a big wave of Matt's favorite soda. The third commercial shows two boys being sucked into a video game. When his meal is done, Matt will usually grab a snack or two to munch on while he continues to watch his shows . . . and favorite commercials.

15

Each day at school, Matt eats lunch with his friends, Riley and Jake. At the school cafeteria, Matt always buys two chocolate milks to drink with his lunch (lasagna is his favorite), and always finishes his meal with an ice cream sandwich. Because Matt eats a much bigger lunch than most of the other kids, the women who work in the cafeteria know him well and greet him by name. They often thank him for liking their food so much. On most days, after finishing his own lunch, Matt eats whatever food Riley and Jake don't want. They are picky eaters and usually leave lots of stuff for Matt to finish off.

Each day, Matt usually gets hungry between meals so he likes to snack. In fact, Matt's whole family likes to snack, so the pantry is usually jam packed with goodies. Matt has a real sweet tooth, so his favorite snacks are cookies, marshmallows, cupcakes, or a few chocolate candy bars washed down with a glass of soda. Matt likes grape soda the best, although he also really likes orange soda or even just regular cola. When Matt has done especially well on a test at school, he is rewarded with a snack from his dad's special "stash" of pastries from the corner bakery.

Matt even snacks while he's out about town. When he's at the mall with his mom, Matt always makes a stop at the food court. There, she and Matt usually devour an entire large pepperoni pizza (his other favorite food), and then they both eat an ice cream cone with two-scoops. His parents have a sweet tooth, too. If they are in a hurry that day, Matt will just get a basket of French fries and a large soda to eat and drink while shopping. He especially loves grocery shopping with his mom, since they always visit the baked goods section for a jumbo cookie to eat while they fill their cart. He is completely unaware of the "Nutrition Facts" printed on most food labels. Whenever and wherever he and his family shop, Matt usually finds some kind of snack. Even at the drugstore check out counter he cannot resist a bar of his favorite chocolate candy. Neither can his dad.

Matt and his family eat out at restaurants a lot, too. As you can probably tell, Matt's favorite type of food is Italian, which he eats at least four times a week. Matt usually orders lasagna since, besides being the yummiest, the restaurant serves a really big portion along with all of the bread sticks he can eat. Even Matt himself cannot believe that he is able to finish such a big piece of lasagna all at once, but it just tastes so good! After looking at Matt's empty dinner plate with pride, his mom orders him a nice big dessert. In fact, everyone in Matt's family gets a dessert so that they can share with one another and sample the restaurant's many different treats. It's so hard to decide on just one, after all.

Other than eating, Matt's favorite activity is playing video games. He has a really large game collection, thanks to his weekly allowance, and he spends hours every day sitting in front of his video game system. Many of Matt's friends ride bikes and play around the neighborhood after school, but Matt would rather sit at his computer at home, play his video games, or just watch TV. There's always something good on, and his parents don't seem to mind.

Matt doesn't do exercise of any kind. Since he's heavy, it's just too hard because he runs out of breath quickly. Exercise also makes him sweat a lot and get all wet and sticky. Whenever Matt can take a shortcut, he does! When there are stairs to climb, he always looks around to see if there is an elevator he can take, instead. Elevators are much easier than walking up a flight of stairs, after all.

At dinnertime, Matt's mom will make one of her many specialties. Matt especially loves her homemade macaroni and cheese, although he likes her southern fried chicken with extra buttery mashed potatoes a lot, too. And, of course, Matt's family believes that no dinner is complete without some kind of dessert, and he always hopes for something—anything—from that yummy corner bakery.

CHAPTER 2

The Skinny on Being Heavy

Because Matt weighs more than he should, he often deals with problems that people at a healthier weight do not. For example, his body often feels uncomfortable. Even if he's not doing too much, he can easily get hot and sweaty—even when other people in the same room are perfectly comfortable. Also, his feet and back hurt if he walks too much. Because he gets tired very easily, it's hard for him to go to fun places like the zoo or to carnivals with his friends. He just doesn't have the energy to keep up with his pals who do not weigh as much.

Matt is bigger—much bigger—than a lot of the other kids at school. This makes him feel "different," and feel bad about himself. He often secretly wishes that he did not weigh so much, and that his body looked like "normal" kids his age. Thinking about this sometimes makes Matt feel really sad. When he's feeling this way, Matt's mom makes him one of her special vanilla milkshakes to cheer him up. And it does.

More than anything, Matt hates to shop for clothes. He has a really hard time finding clothes that fit him, and he usually has to shop at a special store for "big people." Matt likes all of the trendy fashions and wants to dress "cool" like the other kids at school, but he just can't find those styles in his size. Most of the time, Matt just buys whatever fits—whether he likes it or not—and hopes he does not get teased by the other kids.

In fact, Matt has learned the hard way that some people can be unkind and downright mean. He often hears the other kids at school joke or snicker about his heavy weight as he's walking by, or when he's eating lunch in the cafeteria. The really mean kids even tease him by calling him names like "Fat Matt," which hurts his feelings. Sometimes, Matt goes home and cries when people call him names and laugh at him. Those are times when Matt especially wishes that he wasn't so very heavy.

Matt's friends, Riley and Jake, are really nice. They eat lunch with him and sometimes come over to play video games with him after school. But those are Matt's only true friends. The other boys and girls at school don't play with Matt because he looks different and doesn't participate in team sports or other extracurricular activities. He also doesn't play with the neighborhood kids since they're always outside riding bikes, which Matt can't do very well. Sometimes, Matt feels lonely and wishes that he did have more friends to have fun with. Feeling different has made Matt too shy to try and change anything, so every day after school he just does the same old thing in the house.

Because Matt's weight is well above where it should be, his pediatrician, Dr. Franklin, is very concerned. At his last visit, Dr. Franklin tells Matt that if he doesn't change his habits and lose some weight that really bad things can happen to his body. Matt is curious, so Dr. Franklin explains how he's at high risk for serious health problems, such as high blood pressure, high cholesterol, and even type 2 diabetes! That all sounds really scary to Matt . . . and to his Mom and Dad who are understandably worried about the doctor's warning.

CHAPTER 3

Taking Control—Getting Healthy

Matt and his parents are troubled about the bad things Dr. Franklin says can happen if he doesn't lose weight. Matt thinks long and hard about Dr. Franklin's serious health warnings, and even logs onto the Internet with his dad to learn more about the obesity-related health problems his doctor talked about. Matt doesn't like what he learns. In fact, it scares the bejeezers out of him—and with good reason. It turns out that type 2 diabetes—a potentially life threatening condition—is becoming epidemic among overweight children these days. He also learns that type 2 diabetes can cause heart disease, kidney failure . . . and even blindness!

That night Matt has a serious talk with his parents about his weight problem. They all quickly recognize that being overweight has caused so many needless problems in Matt's life. With that realization, Matt decides there and then that it is up to *him* to take control of his life, lose weight, and get healthy. **For the first time in his life, Matt knows that HE has the power to make the changes that will help him look and feel better!** Matt's parent's are extremely excited that he has decided to get healthy, and promise to do what they can to help him reach his goal. They also commit to making healthy lifestyle changes right along with him!

The next day, Matt eats breakfast as he does each morning. However, rather than pancakes with syrup, bacon or donuts, Matt asks his mother for some wheat toast with low-fat and low-sugar peanut butter, a low-fat yogurt and a cup of fruit cocktail packed in juice, not syrup. Matt has done his homework on healthy eating and his mother is happy to oblige. To Matt's surprise, it all tastes pretty good. Thereafter, even though it is sometimes hard to resist the high calorie, sugary foods he loves, Matt makes nutritious breakfast choices that include things like whole grain cereals with low-fat milk and fresh fruit, oatmeal with raisins, and egg white omelets with lean ham and sliced tomatoes.

Matt and his family also start eating breakfast together every day rather than in front of the TV. Matt doesn't care that he misses his favorite shows, or his favorite commercials, since he enjoys the quality time with his folks. Anyway, Matt had seen that funny hamburger a million times it seems, and he knows all of the jokes by heart. This has also stopped Matt from craving fast food as he heads off for school in the morning.

At the school cafeteria, Matt switches from buying two chocolate milks to just one low-fat white milk, and now chooses the healthiest lunch item available—usually a grilled chicken sandwich. He's sure to avoid anything that's fried or has a lot of sauce and cheese. He also stops eating so much mayonnaise, using mustard or ketchup instead—even on his grilled chicken sandwiches! Also, instead of an ice cream sandwich as his sweet treat at the end of lunch, he now eats a low-fat frozen yogurt bar. It actually tastes just as good. The cafeteria workers are very pleased with Matt's healthier choices. Matt also learns to satisfy himself with his own meal, and stops grazing on his friends' leftovers. It's hard at first as old habits are hard to break, after all. But soon Matt feels full enough with just his own healthier lunch selections.

Matt still gets hungry between meals, but his snack choices are MUCH better. Even though they can be really hard for Matt to resist, rather than sugary treats he now selects healthier foods that still taste really good. Everything from pretzels to low-fat cheese and crackers, nuts and raisins, veggies and dip, to fruit smoothies are fair game. Matt's mom now keeps lots of healthy stuff in the pantry so that it's easier for him, and her, to make good choices. Also, instead of soda, Matt drinks water . . . and a lot of low-fat milk since it's loaded with calcium that helps build strong bones. He is thinking of trying out for the football team next season, and athletes need strong bones, after all.

Now when Matt has to go out shopping, he's sure to grab a quick healthy snack like an apple or pretzels before he leaves the house so that he's not tempted to eat junk food everywhere he goes. He knows the temptations will still be, well, everywhere, but with a tummy full of healthy food it's much easier for him to maintain his willpower and resist those temptations. And when it gets hard, his mom or dad is there to help him stay in control. Getting healthy has been a real team effort. They also now read the "Nutrition Facts" printed on food labels, which helps them know exactly what they're buying and ensures they are not tricked by labels with false or misleading health claims.

Matt's favorite food is still lasagna and he still orders it at restaurants sometimes, but now he orders a salad appetizer with a low-fat dressing on the side (and is sure to not use all of it). He also eats only a small amount of the huge portion of lasagna the restaurant serves and brings the rest home to have, in moderation, another time. As for dessert, he still gets that, too. But now, it's usually a bowl of fresh berries with just a touch of whipped cream on the side. Matt's mom and dad order different fruit bowls or frozen sorbet so they can still share with one another.

After school, Matt has been heading outside to play in the neighborhood with his friends instead of just sitting at home and playing video games. He still loves video games, but his mom now only lets him play a few hours each week to encourage him to do other activities. Matt's dad bought him a new bicycle, and he's been practicing every day with it. He can even keep up with Jonathan and Ross, who both live on Matt's street and are two of the best athletes in the whole neighborhood! Being able to keep up with other kids really makes Matt feel good about himself.

Since Matt started riding his bike after school, other activities seem to have also gotten easier for him. During PE at school, Matt's been playing soccer and baseball with the other boys. It was hard at first, but every time he plays it gets easier and easier . . . and he gets better and better. He even hit his first home run! Matt still sweats a lot and gets all wet and sticky, but he doesn't mind since he's having so much fun.

At dinnertime, Matt's mom has bunch of new low-fat and low-calorie specialties that the family enjoys as much as her other, less healthy recipes. Fish, chicken breast, and lean cuts of beef and pork are now staples in their home, and Matt's mom has learned how to prepare these foods in a really healthy, but tasty way. She even found recipes for some really healthy desserts because, as you now know, Matt's family feels that no dinner is complete without some kind of dessert . . . even if it's a nutritious one.

CHAPTER 4

Just Desserts

Since Matt has taken control of his weight, many areas of his life have improved. For one thing, his feet and back no longer hurt when he walks, which allows him to do many more fun things with his friends, like walking to the park to play, or spending hours at the state fair. He even joined a boys' club and went on a hike! Matt's made many new friends in the boys' club.

Matt's new smaller size also allows him to shop at the same stores as his friends, and he now has a bunch of new and really cool clothes that he's proud to wear. This has gotten him noticed a lot more—even by Stephanie, the prettiest girl at school. Matt couldn't help but grin from ear to ear when she told him she liked his new look.

The days of Matt being teased about his clothes are long gone! In fact, the same kids who used to call him "Fat Matt" now ask him to play sports with them during recess. It turns out that, after dropping the excess weight, Matt is a really good athlete and is always a first pick for teams. This has increased Matt's confidence so much that even his grades have improved! Now, instead of trying to not be noticed in class, he's among the first to raise his hand to answer questions from the teacher. Matt's parents have never been so proud of him.

At Matt's next visit with Dr. Franklin six months later, he is very nervous about what the doctor will say about his health. After all, his last visit didn't go very well. But, when Dr. Franklin walks in the examination room, he takes one look at Matt and exclaims, "Wow, you look fantastic!" It is obvious to Dr. Franklin that Matt has lost a lot of weight, and that he looks and feels healthier. The doctor tells Matt how proud he is that he made sensible lifestyle changes that took the weight off at a safe pace, and that he's improved his over-all health condition. Dr. Franklin is also pleased with Matt's parents for supporting, and joining, his efforts, and for their own noticeable weight loss achievements.

Now that Matt and his family are down to a healthy weight and know what to do to keep it that way, everyone is healthier . . . and everyone is definitely happier.

After years making poor lifestyle choices that made Matt's body feel uncomfortable and caused him to feel bad about himself, Matt is extremely proud of his weight loss accomplishment. This newfound confidence has improved nearly every area of his life.

Each night before Matt goes to sleep, he approaches a mirror and looks himself in the eye and declares, **"If I can do this, I can do anything!"**

And he can.

PARENTS' SECTION

Story Discussion

Parents, immediately after reading this story with your child you are encouraged to discuss it with him using the following questions as a guide. This will ensure he recognizes the important themes portrayed in the story as it relates to:

- Common negative cultural influences that lead to bad choices

- Challenges that overweight and obese children often face on a daily basis related to physical, emotional, and social functions

- Behavioral changes that can be made <u>right now</u> to take control

- Specific tangible benefits that may be realized by taking control

Such dialogue is truly the first step in getting your child motivated to take charge of his weight and, in doing so, his life.

Discussion Questions

- Why was Matt's overweight condition not entirely his fault?

- Before Matt's visit to the doctor, why were the breakfasts he ate so bad? What are some good breakfast choices to make?

- Why shouldn't Matt eat his meals in front of the TV? Do you think it makes him mindlessly eat more than he should?

- What was Matt doing wrong in the school cafeteria before he decided to lose weight and get healthy?

- Is portion control important, or is just eating nutritious foods enough?

- What should Matt choose as healthy snack options in between meals?

- What can Matt do to avoid mindless eating and snacking while out and about?

- What are at least three good choices Matt can make when eating at a restaurant?

- Why do you think Matt's mother restricted his use of video games? Do you agree with that decision?

- If there are both stairs and an elevator, which should Matt choose? Why?

- Why is it important for Matt's family to support his desire to make lifestyle changes?

- Do you think Matt's mom should buy groceries and cook meals that can help his effort to lose weight and stay healthy?

- Do you think it matters if Matt's mom and dad eat healthy foods with him?

- Why was Matt's body uncomfortable when he was heavy and what couldn't he do? Why?

- Should Matt's mom give him a vanilla shake to cheer him up when he's feeling sad? What else could she do to cheer him up?

- Why didn't Matt like to shop for clothes before losing weight?

- Did Matt's feelings ever get hurt at school when he was heavy?

- What was Matt's doctor concerned about? Why?

- After Matt lost weight, what are some good things that happened in his life? Would these things have happened if he had not lost weight?

HEALTHY LIVING TIP SHEET

Below are few of the many ways you can help your child take control of his health RIGHT NOW and start making positive lifestyle changes. Your child has nothing but weight to lose, and nothing but health and happiness to gain! Help your child get on the right track today with this helpful—and potentially life-saving—advice. As always, before you start, please consult a physician about which activities are safe for your child.

- **Unplug.** Turn off the TV at snack time. Studies show that those who watch TV while eating consume higher fat and saltier snacks; and eat less fruit and vegetables. Increased TV viewing correlates with higher rates of obesity in kids.

- **Empower him.** Involve children in the planning, shopping, and preparing of meals and snacks. The more involved the child is, the more familiar and accepting he will be of healthy meal planning.

- **Switch it up.** Small modifications can pay- big dividends. Substituting one percent milk for whole milk saves calories and fat, without sacrificing nutrition. Use mustard and ketchup on burgers instead of mayonnaise.

- **Dish it up.** Plate entrées in the kitchen instead of serving family style. Portion size counts as much as food selection. Offer seconds on salad and other vegetables.

- **Chuck the chips.** Buy healthy snacks instead of fatty chips and dips. Offer baby carrots with a fat-free ranch dressing, pretzels, grapes, and baked tortilla chips with bean dip or salsa.

- **Order "on the side."** When ordering at restaurants, teach kids to order salad dressing and other condiments and sauces "on the side." Don't let bread be an eating utensil for butter.

- **Eliminate empty calories.** A 20-ounce soda has at least 10 teaspoons of added sugar and no nutritional value. Encourage water instead.

- **Get moving.** Get everyone off the couch and take a fun family walk each night after dinner. Take a hike. Put on the radio and dance! As a start, ask your child to walk briskly whenever and wherever he walks. Be sure to praise your child whenever he chooses to be active and play.

- **Be flexible.** There are no "forbidden foods." All foods can fit into a healthy diet . . . in moderation. Dedicate a day each week to cook an "old favorite" dish that your family loves but no longer eats on a regular basis.

- **Educate.** Read food labels, starting with the number of servings in the package. When you know that important piece of information, the rest of the numbers, including calories, grams of fat, protein and carbohydrate, sodium and sugar grams, make sense.

- **Set an example.** Challenge your child to set a fitness goal, and you set one too: for example, walking five miles; doing three sets of twenty sit ups; joining a karate class to work toward your green belt. The possibilities are endless. Reserve at least one day each weekend dedicated to fun family fitness activities.

- **Start early.** Your child is never too young to be concerned about lasting health issues. Children as young as two should follow the same nutrition guidelines as adults. If they don't, it's quite possible they can later be faced with high cholesterol and/or heart disease as a result.

- **Prepare.** Create a nurturing, non-intimidating environment for active play both inside and outside the home. Provide opportunities for your child to safely climb, run, and jump to develop muscle strength and bone density.

- **Get creative.** Consider requiring that when your child watches television, he has to do some kind of exercise or physical movement during commercials. While watching a movie on video or DVD, turn it off every thirty minutes and ask him to dance, jump rope, or do crunches for five to ten minutes. Reward success. Ensure monetary allowance is also based on helpful yet healthy activities such as vacuuming, walking the dog, shoveling snow, and raking leaves.

ABOUT THE AUTHOR

Child health advocate and award-winning author Merilee A. Kern is the founder and CEO of Healthy Kids' Catalog (www.HealthyKidsCatalog.com)—an online storefront offering "Solutions that Foster Healthy Children." Merilee is also Editor-in-Chief of *WEIGHT-WISE KIDS*, a free monthly electronic newsletter that "serves up" child health-related news, advice, and information, and serves as an editorial contributor for other media outlets nationwide.

In addition to having worked in the billion-dollar weight loss industry for many years, Merilee is also a life-long fitness enthusiast and a former body-building champion twice over, having previously won the titles of "Miss South Florida" and "Miss Palm Coast." She has participated in sports throughout her youth, and has spent all of her adult years devoted to good nutrition, fitness, and healthy living—a lifestyle that she, together with her husband whom she met at the gym, now impart on their two young children.

Merilee also owns and operates Kern Communications (www.kerncommunications.com)—a boutique public relations and marketing communications agency. She earned her Master of Business Administration and Bachelor of Science degree, both with a marketing specialty, from Nova Southeastern University in Fort Lauderdale, Florida.

Lightning Source UK Ltd.
Milton Keynes UK
UKOW07f1940110116

266121UK00002B/21/P